For Sukie
&
thanks to Chris

THE RED DREAD

THE
RED
DREAD

Thump thump   thump thump

TOM MORGAN-JONES

thump thump thump thump thump thump

thump thump thump thump thump thump
thump thump thump thump thump thump

THUMP THUMP
THUMP THUMP THU...

Thump thump

Has anybody seen my shoes?

First published in 2018 in Great Britain by
The Bucket List, an imprint of Barrington Stoke
18 Walker Street, Edinburgh, EH3 7LP

www.bucketlistbooks.co.uk

Text & Illustrations © 2018 Tom Morgan-Jones

A CIP catalogue record for this book is available
from the British Library upon request

ISBN: 978-1-911370-05-5

Printed in Turkey

THE
BUCKET
LIST